Runners' Fairy Tales

Contents

Dedication

THANK YOU TO THE SLO ROADRUNNERS FOR MAKING RUNNING SUCH AN ENJOYABLE EXPERIENCE! (ESPECIALLY THOSE LATE-NIGHT SPEEDWORK SESSIONS WITH NO LIGHTS WHERE THE SEEDS FOR MANY OF THESE TALES WERE ORIGINALLY PLANTED!)

Hansel and Gretel Go for a Run

Once upon a time there were two distance runners named Hansel and Gretel. They worked out at a track near their house. Every day they ran round and round the perfectly smooth, all-weather polyurethane surface adding up mile after mile until each became local legends on their Strava segments. The place was old and clunky, but it was familiar, and it was theirs.

Occasionally they would see people running on the streets or sidewalks nearby.

"Why would anyone do that?" asked Gretel. "I like it right here!"

"Seriously," Hansel agreed. "We have everything we need!"

Gretel stopped running and pointed to a dilapidated plastic structure at the far corner. "Well," she sighed. "Everything except that."

Hansel considered the faded green walls and winced. “Ugh, that disgusting outhouse!”

Given its proximity to a university campus, an AM-PM minimart, and a Bev Mo surplus outlet store, the outhouse was always filled with all manner of horrible leavings, the aftereffects of too much alcohol and too many microwavable bean burritos. It emanated a perpetual cloud of noxious gasses.

“So gross,” Gretel said.

“And it hasn’t been emptied in months!”

“At least you don’t have to sit in it!” Gretel shuddered. “At the track, at the starting line of races ... why do all the running outhouses have to be so nasty? What I wouldn’t give for something that flushes!”

That night the two runners could not keep the images of filthy outhouses from their nightmares. The next morning when the sun rose, Gretel texted her friend, “We cannot run at the track anymore. We must find a better place with a nicer toilet. We will search through the woods today!”

"But what if we get lost?” Hansel replied.

“We won’t!” said Gretel. “We’ll wear our Garmins. If we have to, we can use the GPS to get back home.”

And so, the two of them went off into the woods and left the filthy outhouse behind.

They ran stride for stride always keeping their eyes open for a nice track with clean facilities. But after a few hours, once their digestive urges began to increase, nothing could be found. Still, they pressed on.

"Remember that half we ran in Ojai?" Gretel asked. "The port-a-potty was so full it was overflowing!"

Hansel winced. "Or at the start of Boston when the line was over an hour long? Miserable!"

"I about peed myself!"

"You know, all this talk about bathrooms has gotten me thinking ... I probably shouldn't have had those extra two coconut-almond-spinach smoothies before we left today."

"What? You have a bladder the size of an acorn and you drank extra fluids?"

"Well, what about you? All you can eat sushi for dinner last night with your advanced, tenacious runner's trots?"

Gretel's intestines gurgled. "Yeah. Bad choice." She looked around at the trees and scrub, the afternoon shadows turning the branches to grasping claws. "There are no bathrooms out here. And I just can't squat in these creepy bushes!"

As time passed, they became more and more desperate. At last, poor Hansel and Gretel knew they must return to their disgusting outhouse or night would fall and they would surely explode. But which way to go? The trails all looked the same in the evening dimness!

“Are we ... are we lost?” Gretel asked, clenching her protesting glutes.

Hansel swiveled his head while tightly crossing his legs. He pushed buttons on his Garmin, trying to open his GPS. But the screen was frozen! “Oh no! There is no signal this deep in the forest!”

“This is terrible!”

“Gretel,” whispered Hansel in growing distress, “what will we do?”

She did not know what to say. Each moment the pressure in her bowels grew and grew! "I'm not sure but I feel a fartlek coming on!"

At that moment, Gretel saw a small light shining far away. Could it be someone's cabin this deep in the woods? "We must find out!" she cried. "Maybe whoever lives there is kind and will let us use the bathroom."

The two runners sped toward the light as fast as their Nike Alphaflys could carry them.

When they got closer, they could not believe their eyes! If you can imagine – emerging from the gloom, a building warmly lit with welcoming lights. Two sturdy blue doors, each emblazoned with the magical word, “restroom” stood as if waiting just for them. What a wonderous sight to see!

“Gretel!” Hansel cried out, amazed. But before Gretel could reply, they were both sprinting ahead, loosening their Rabbit FKTs, and unbuckling their matching Lululemon run belts. And when they reached the doors .... they were unlocked!

Welcoming light pooled around their feet as they pushed open the doors. Inside there were sinks so spotless they sparkled, fresh towels neatly waiting, and silver faucets that gleamed like a 400 lumen Fenix high performance running headlamp! The air freshener wafted the alluring scent of Tiger Balm Ultra pain relief ointment and hidden speakers invited them in with music lilting at precisely 180 beats per minute.

And there, in the far corner, a beautiful, squeaky-clean toilet ... a functioning, real life, pressure-assisted, self-flushing wonder!

“There’s no grime, no graffiti!” exclaimed Gretel.

“And no vomitous stench or mystery sludge!” laughed Hansel.

With that they rushed inside their respective rooms and, ahhhh, let nature come full force! The joyous sounds of their relief echoed throughout the land!

After several flushes, most done out of sheer joy, Gretel was washing her hands in the glorious sink and drying with freshly folded towels when she spotted something peculiar by the door. It appeared to be some sort of vending machine. She approached, curious. There, inside, was every type of energy gel imaginable; all flashing with the word, "free"!

"Hansel," she called through the wall. "Come quick! Come see! By the door, a ... a ..."

"An energy gel dispenser!" Hansel interrupted. "There's one in my side, too!" He pushed button B3 and out came a pouch of his favorite Salted Caramel Gu. He tried another, C1, and scored a Vanilla Bean. "And they're free! They really are!"

Gretel began pushing buttons as well. The machine released packet after packet of Maurten, SiS, Huma, Rocktane, and B-Line Beet+Mango racing fuel. "It's a miracle," she giggled, stuffing her far too small running shorts pockets.

After some time of this, they both stumbled outside with their respective hauls, hundreds of dollars of gels in their hands.

"I've already eaten two," Hansel grinned while slurping another. "But I sure could use something to wash them down." He looked about, hoping there might be a drinking fountain. Instead, his eyes fell upon a row of foldable plastic tables. "What's that?" he asked, pointing. "It's like a marathon finish line."

The two runners moved closer. They found trays of sliced oranges, piles of half bananas, tiny bags of salted pretzels, and dozens of little plastic cups half filled with Gatorade Endurance, lemon lime flavor.

Hansel picked up two cups and drank. "Why are they always only half full?" he asked.

"And why is it always lemon lime flavor?" Gretel observed, joining him.

At the far end of the tables, beyond the display of salted watermelon Cliff Blocks and Honey Stinger Carmel Waffles sat a pile of carefully folded foil space blankets.

"And why are there always space blankets?" the two laughed in unison.

They spent an hour or more resting, eating, hydrating, and using those awesome restrooms just because they could. Soon it was extremely late and very very dark.

"My GPS still doesn't work," said Hansel.

"Mine either," confirmed Gretel. "But we'll be able to find our way in the morning, right?"

The chill of the night air began to prickle through their still sweaty clothes and the strange sounds of the forest surrounded them.

"This is the first time I've been glad for a space blanket," Hansel said, forcing an uneasy smile as he grabbed one for each of them. "Guess we'll be spending the night here."

"It's just one night. Really only a few hours until dawn. Maybe we can get a couple of hours of sleep and start out early?"

"Yes. The earlier the better."

But the skittering flitters from the darkened branches and the snapping clomps from the forest floor combined with the 2x caffeine shots in their gels and chews to keep any type of sleep far far away.

As the blackness continued to thicken and the ground became more and more uncomfortable, Gretel sighed. "The clean bathrooms are nice and all, but I sure wish we'd ran at our old track today instead of coming out here!"

Hansel agreed. "I'm always ready to run 26.2 miles for half a banana but right now I'd rather be done with my ice bath and be posting screenshots of my Strava mileage on Instagram to annoy all our nonrunning friends."

"Do we have nonrunning friends?" Gretel asked.

"There's got to be at least one out there, right?" He paused, thinking. "But more to the point. I'd rather be there, stinky outhouse and all, than here in this well stocked, but creepy forest!"

And so, the hours crept by, slower than a sag wagon on senior marathon day at the retirement village. Finally, after what seemed an eternity, the first rays of sun began peeking through the treetops.

Hansel stood and stretched. "Are you about ready to go?"

"I don't know." Gretel looked longingly at the bathrooms. "I ate and drank so much last night I'm afraid to stray too far from the flush!"

"And I hate to leave all this Gatorade and snack food. But we can't just stay here forever, can we?"

"No," Gretel stated. "We should leave right away." She hesitated. "Well, maybe after one more trip to the bathroom."

"And breakfast! We should stay long enough for breakfast. But then, yes, we leave immediately!"

After three rounds of Honey Stinger waffles, bananas, and half glasses of Gatorade combined with four trips to the commode to empty, flush, and wash, Hansel and Gretel left promptly at about 10:45. They had trouble running due to the added weight from their filled pockets, belts, stomachs, and intestines. Barely maintaining 12-minute miles it seemed to take them forever to find their way back out of the forest. But when they did their hearts were brimming with joy.

“Look,” pointed Hansel. “It’s our old track!”

“And better,” cheered Gretel. “It’s the disgusting outhouse!” And with that she broke into the closest thing to a sprint she’d managed all day, delighted once again to be in her familiar, albeit vile, surroundings.

And they peed happily ever after.

Jack and Jill

Jack and Jill went up the hill to get to the starting line of a Revel marathon with a total descent of 10,000 feet along a 7.2% grade.

Jack fell down because, not surprisingly, his quads weren't properly trained for such a downhill run, and broke his crown, his right 5th metatarsal, his IT band, and developed left Achilles' tendinopathy.

And Jill came tumbling after.

Up Jack got, and home did trot as fast as he could caper, because one doesn't quit in the middle of a race no matter what happens.

Soaked in ice and popped a few Advil and wrapped himself in a Nike Pro Advanced Recovery compression suit while signing up for his next race on the following Saturday!

Goldilocks and the Three Pairs (of Running Shoes)

Once upon a time, there was a young runner named Goldilocks. One day while sipping a kale smoothie at the country club fitness center following her once weekly yoga blast class and full body massage, she noticed an advertisement on the high-definition monitor behind the bar. Not believing what she saw, she blinked and looked again. Sure enough, there they were. The words "House of Tiffany, Exclusive Boutique."

She fluffed her golden trusses and turned to the barista. "Excuse me," she asked in a voice tinged with excitement, pointing to the screen. "What is that?"

"That's a 10k. Starts tomorrow morning in Founders Park, circles along the waterfront, and ends outside the House of Tiffany clothing store. Should be a nice little workout."

"Exclusive boutique," Goldilocks corrected. "Not 'clothing store.' This is not a Walmart! House of Tiffany, Exclusive Boutique caters to only the most discriminating clientele, like me!" With that she took a final swallow of her green drink, touched up her nude pink lip liner, picked up her Gucci bag, and rushed out of the room. She had no idea what a 10k was, but if it involved House of Tiffany, Exclusive Boutique, it had to be extravagant and include only the most refined people!

The next morning Goldilocks arrived at Founders Park ready for a trip to the elite shopping experience of her dreams. Expecting it to be, as the barista described, a "nice little workout," she came in her yoga best. CHNOOI zippered sports bra, PULNCD soft stretch yoga band running shorts, Rainbow Stripe cashmere light sweater pant, and Vibram VI-B Fitness yoga shoe, nails freshly buffed and coordinated bangle earrings, just enough to sparkle. To her dismay there were no limousines lined up to parade the participants to the boutique. Instead, she saw a throng of spandex clad people milling about a variety of tables and booths.

Goldilocks fluffed her curls and wrinkled her nose in confusion.

"You look lost," a stranger said. "If you're part of the 10k you need to start right over there at the registration table. Get yourself a bib."

"Excuse me, a what?" Goldilocks asked. "A bib? Did you say a bib?"

"You're here for the 10k?"

"To House of Tiffany, Exclusive Boutique, right?"

The stranger nodded and pointed again to the registration table. Goldilocks hesitantly complied.

“Welcome,” said the man behind the table. “Let’s get you set up.” He pointed to three stacks of rectangular papers, each with a number on them. “Which are you?”

“I don’t understand,” said Goldilocks.

"These are the 10k bibs. The neon yellow are our charity bibs. The slate gray are our regular bibs. And the teal ones are for our elite athletes."

She looked at the three types. "Oh my. The neon bibs are too bright! The gray bibs are too dull! But the teal bibs are just right! And they match the highlights on my nails!"

"I'm sorry," said the man. "Those are exclusively for our elite athletes. Unless your name is Sara Hall, Jordan Hasay, or Eliud Kipchoge then those are not for you."

"But I need one for the 10k," she stated. "And you can't expect me to be mismatched!"

"I'm sorry," replied the man.

Goldilocks stepped back, shocked and a little disappointed. But undeterred, when the man began helping another participant, she snatched one of the teal elite bibs and walked away! That did not make the man very happy.

Wandering through the crowd she looked for the limousines or shuttles or whatever was there to take her to the House of Tiffany, Exclusive Boutique. Finally, she asked a young lady doing active stretches along the curb. "Excuse me. Can you tell me where the 10k starts?"

"Right over there by that inflatable archway," the stretching lady answered. "But girlfriend, tell me you aren't going to run in that zippered sports bra! You're going to chafe something fierce! And those shoes? Oh no no no! Blisters just waiting to happen!"

"Running? There's running involved?"

"Yes, indeed! But no finishing at House of Tiffany, Exclusive Boutique for you unless we get you fixed up, and quick!" She grabbed Goldilocks by the hand and dragged her toward to cluster of support and product tables. "Work your way through there. Starting at the one with first aid and personal items. What type of lube do you use?"

"I, uh," Goldilocks stammered. "I've never had to lube, at least not in public."

"Well, find yourself something that works, slather it all sorts of ways under that zipper, and then go on down to the shoe table." And with that, the lady went back to her stretching.

Goldilocks opened a container of plain Vaseline and rubbed it between her fingers. "This lube is too slimy," she said. She then shook some Anti-Monkey Butt powder onto her palm. "This lube is too dry!" Finally, she picked up a stick of Squirrel's Nut Butter Anti-Chafe Salve and tried it. "This one," she smiled, "is just right!" Thinking the table was filled with free swag she slipped it into her pocket and walked away.

This did not make the table's proprietor very happy.

Moving through the booths, Goldilocks saw one with piles of new shoes. "I certainly don't want blisters on my feet," she said to herself. "That might mess up my pedi!" So, she tried on a pair of Saucony Fastwitch 9 racing flats. "Oh goodness," she winced. "These shoes are too hard!" She tried a pair of On Cloudstratus 2 shoes. "And these? Nope! Way too soft!" Finally, she found a pair of ASICS Gel-Kayanos, slipped them on her feet and, ahhh, they were just right! Tying them tight, and thinking they were also part of her swag, she walked away from the table.

This did not make the proprietor very happy.

Properly lubed and shod, Goldilocks headed to the inflatable arch with a giant sign emblazoned with the word "Start." Founder's Park, she knew was at the top of the hill, just above House of Tiffany, Exclusive Boutique. In fact, looking through the Aspen trees she could see it's welcoming tile roof and sparkling clean windows. As the crow flies, it really wasn't that far. Of course, that was straight down the side of the hill, rocks, trees, and all!

It was then she spotted the route for the 10k displayed on a map near the starting line. "What is this?" she gasped. "It looks like they expect us to go in the opposite direction! Away from House of Tiffany, Exclusive Boutique! Away from my shopping! And not only that, but they are also all going down to the waterfront before finally coming back this way! That's over six miles!

Why go all that way when we could simply head down 1st street and hang a left. Even walking that would only take 10 minutes!"

A voice came over the loudspeaker, "Welcome to our 10k race! Please make sure your bibs are on and proceed to the starting area!"

Goldilocks remembered her teal elite bib and pinned it to her clothing. She wanted to make certain she'd get into House of Tiffany, Exclusive Boutique once she arrived. But she didn't think going all the way to the waterfront was such a good idea! What if they wouldn't let her shop until after everyone made that long trek? That would be awful!

Jumping up and down she began waving her arms and shouting. "Wait, wait everybody! Don't run off the way they are saying! That way is too long! The House of Tiffany, Exclusive Boutique is just down there! True, going straight down the side of the hill is too short. But going down 1st street and taking a left is just right! Follow me and let's all go shopping!"

At that point she heard the voice of the registration man complaining to a race official, "Somebody's been stealing my elite bibs!"

This was followed by another voice complaining, "Somebody's been stealing my lubes!"

A third voice added, “Somebody’s been stealing my shoes, and look! She’s right there!”

The race official looked straight at Goldilocks and the group of them started her way!

Goldilocks saw them coming. “I just want to go shopping at the House of Tiffany, Exclusive Boutique!"

"This is a 10k road race. It's a run! Not a shopping trip!" The race official growled. "The finish line just happens to be at the street outside the shop!"

Only then did she realize something had gone terribly wrong! "I'm so sorry!" she said. Leaving behind the bib, the lube, and the shoes, Goldilocks ran down 1st Street, hung a left, and never went to a 10k again!

Rubber Duckie (The Ice Bath Song)

Rubber duckie you're the one
You make ice baths lots of fun
Rubber duckie I like to get cold with you

Rubber duckie I must confess
When the ice hits I'm a mess!
Rubber duckie can you please bring a sweater, too?

Oh, after runs when I make my way to the tubby
I find you ready with enough ice to make me go buggy

Rub-a-dub-a-dubby

Rubber duckie I've been told
That revenge is best served cold
Rubber duckie, I'm becoming afraid of you...

Oh, after runs when I make my way to the tubby
Your twisted grin and evil eyes make me wish I'd taken karate!

Rub-a-dub-a-dubby

Rubber duckie, this is cruel
And I'm freezing like a fool
Rubber duckie, won't you please say goodbye?
Rubber duckie, why don't you just die?
Rubber duckie, I don't want to ice with you!

Little Red Running Hood

Once upon a time, there was a young runner who lived in the town of Hopkinton, the starting point of the Boston Marathon which was scheduled to happen very soon.

Whenever she went out for a run, the girl posted selfies all over her social media while wearing a pair of ASICS MetaSpeed Sky flats in performance red, a crimson Lux Performance singlet, a ruby Hourihan hooded cape, and, as an accent, a Nike Aerobill Dri-FIT Featherlight hat, so all her 4,596 followers took to calling her Little Red Running Hood.

One morning, Little Red Running Hood asked her mother if she could run the Boston Marathon with her grandmother as it had been a while since they'd run together.

"That's a good idea," her mother said. “I can get you a charity bib. But remember, your grandmother is a 2:38:33 marathoner and wins her age group in every event she enters! Don’t do anything to slow her down!” So, they packed up her Naked under-shorts running belt with a collection of energy gels, chews, and waffles to take along on her run.

When her supplies were ready, the girl used her Theragun Pro to warm up her legs, used the bathroom for the third time, and put on her MetaSpeeds, singlet, and cape. She then kissed her mother goodbye, used the bathroom one more time, just to be safe, and grabbed her Samsung Galaxy S22 Ultra with a four-camera photography suite as she started for the door.

"Remember, run with Grandma," her mother cautioned. "Don't dawdle along the way and please don't stop to take selfies! The route is dangerous."

"Don't worry, Mom," said Little Red Running Hood. "I'll be careful."

But when Little Red Running Hood met her grandmother near the starting corrals, she pulled her smart phone out from the sweat-resistant pocket in her Sarah Sports Bra. “Grandma, wait! Let’s grab a shot of us with the starting chute in the background!”

Her grandmother interrupted her A-skips and sighed. "Maybe just one, dear, and only if you don't run in the cape. Wind resistance, you know. Once we cross that starting line we need to focus, ok? I promised your mother I'd run with you today and, remember, you promised to keep your mind on the race!"

"I will, Grandma," Little Red said while posing them for the perfect shot. "I promise!" Then she tossed her cape in the charity pile and headed off to the course.

And with her phone vibrating and pinging with comments from her happy followers, the two turned, crossed over the timing mat, and began their journey toward Boston.

Little Red Running Hood did her best to focus as they made their way past George V. Brown and The Spirit of the Marathon statues. Her camera fingers twitched only a little when, at mile two, they proceeded with the other runners past TJ's Food and Spirits. But by the time they'd reached Ashland she could resist no more.

"Oh Grandma, look," Little Red exclaimed. "The old clocktower! I've just got to take a picture!" She stopped in the middle of the road, other racers swerving to get around her, pulled out her phone, held up a peace sign next to her princess grin, and took a selfie.

Grandma stopped. "Red, you promised!"

"It was just one," she rolled her eyes. "My followers expect it! What's the big deal?"

But it wasn't just one. Soon she noticed some lovely roadside flowers. She forgot her promises to her mother and grandmother as she live streamed a message to her fans. This was followed by more shoots in Framingham near the train station and Natick with an amazingly handsome firefighter. Each time her grandmother scolded and each time the girl just shrugged.

On reaching the tunnel of cheers at Wellesley College, Little Red Running Hood was enjoying stopping and taking selfies with each of the Wellesley girls so much, that she didn't notice a dark shadow approaching along the route from behind her...

Suddenly, the sag wagon appeared at her side!

"What are you doing out here?" the driver asked in a voice as friendly as he could muster.

"I'm running the Boston Marathon with my grandma," Little Red pointed to the now highly aggravated elder nearby, "and taking selfies to share with all my followers!"

"Isn't that nice," exclaimed the sag wagon driver. "Take your time. Enjoy yourself! How often do you get to be part of such a prestigious event as this?" But what the driver didn't say was that he got paid extra for every runner who tarried too long that he scooped up in his sag wagon and drove to the finish line. He began to open the door to the back seat...

Grandma grabbed Little Red's arm and pulled her away. "We've got to run, girl! I've never had a DNF, and I don't intend to get one today!" The two hurried away.

"Wait," protested Little Red. "I want to get a picture of that nice driver!"

But her grandmother didn't let go until they were well on their way to Newton.

Little Red Running Hood did her best to ignore her buzzing and pinging phone. But she knew her followers wanted to know her progress. She was worried they might think she had died, or worse, dropped her phone, if they didn't get an update soon. So, once again, she stopped and began streaming at the base of Heartbreak Hill.

Grandma, with hands sternly on her hips, scowled. But before a word could escape her mouth, the sag wagon snuck up from behind and gobbled her up!

Little Red looked about and didn't see her grandmother. "She must have run on ahead," Little Red thought. "I'd better hurry and catch up!" But before she set off, she thought it wise to eat her strawberry Cliff Blocks and nibble on a Honey Stinger waffle. Then she thought her followers might like a picture of her having a little reenergizing picnic halfway up Heartbreak Hill. So, she posed, mouth open, and her treats near her pearly teeth.

The shadow loomed behind her once again. It was the sag wagon!

“Hello again,” said the driver, thinking of the additional money he was about to earn. “It looks like you’ve fallen behind everyone else. Let me give you a ride. You don’t want to be out here when the course closes down, do you?”

Little Red Running Hood smiled politely, “I’m running with my Grandmother. I think she’s just ahead. But thank you for the offer.”

“I really must insist,” said the driver.

“You’re so nice! But I’ll just catch up with Grandma.”

“Enough!” growled the driver. “You can’t catch up with your precious grandmother because she’s already in the sag wagon! Now get in there and join her!”

Little Red inched toward the vehicle and peered into the back seat. “If my grandma is in there why are the windows tinted and closed?”

“The better to hide her embarrassment, my dear,” the driver replied.

“But if she’s really in there, why are the doors closed and locked?” she asked.

"The better to help her rest and stay cool in the air conditioning, my dear," he said.

Just then, Little Red Running Hood saw a hand press against the smokey glass and the vague silhouette of what could have been her grandmother's face right behind it. Little Red looked toward the top of Heartbreak Hill, knowing Grandma must have run on ahead. She would never get into a sag wagon, would she? "But if she's really in there, why is she pressing her hand against the window?"

"The better to have you come in and join her, my dear."

"Oh. Ok. That makes sense." She stepped the rest of the way to the sag wagon. "I'll get in with her!"

The driver laughed, an evil, rasping, maniacal sound, and began unlocking and opening the door.

"But before I do, may I please live stream this moment for my 4,596 social media followers?" She held up her Samsung Galaxy, choosing the close-up lens.

“Live stream?” The driver tried to paste a sincere looking smile on his face. “4,596 witnesses?” He faltered for just a moment as if unsure. “You mean I could go viral?”

In that instant, Little Red Running Hood yanked open the door of the sag wagon. “Grandma, you’re a 2:48:33 marathoner and I’m wearing ASICS Metaspeed Skys with carbon fiber insoles!”

Grandma scurried out of the backseat. “The better to run away from this loser, my dear!”

Together the two sprinted up the hill, past the Citgo sign, and onto Boylston where they crossed the finish line holding hands.

“Oh Grandma, I’m so sorry!” sobbed Little Red Running Hood, "I'll never dawdle or take selfies again."

“There, there, child. You've learned an important lesson. Just remember, there’s a time and a place for everything, even going slow and sharing your world with online followers. Just maybe not during a marathon!”

“Agreed!” laughed Little Red, accepting her finisher’s medal and half a banana from a race volunteer. “Now, let’s see how many likes and comments we received!”

Wee Willie Winkie

Wee Willie Winkie runs through the town!
With headlamp before sunrise
In his in his Lululemon's!
Rapping at the windows!
Crying at the locks!
Why are you still in your beds? We run at 5:00!
Why are you still in your beds? We run at 5:00!

Cinder Fella

Once upon a time there lived a young man named Danny who worked as a sports medicine intern at the prestigious Emerald Track Club. He happily assisted his friend and mentor, Coach Bob, as some of the top athletes in the kingdom trained. Oftentimes Danny would take part in the drills where he was surprised to find he could more than hold his own, even in his old shoes and threadbare gear.

“One of these days,” Danny told Coach Bob, “I’m going to run in the Olympics!”

“I believe in you, Danny.” Coach Bob reassured. “You keep up your training, fight through the hardships, and never give up hope. Sometimes dreams do come true!”

By and by it came to pass that Coach Bob retired and moved to the mountains of Tibet. But training stops for no man. A new leader arrived on the scene. The arrogant, evil, and haughty Coach Tremaine. And with him came his two superstar milers Andy and Driz. Never before or since have there been a pair who behaved so aloof and entitled.

Danny’s happy life took a serious turn for the worse.

“Surely you can’t expect Andy and Driz to train on this track surface!” Coach Tremaine snapped when he first arrived. “This is last year’s model. To be the best, my runners need the best.” He pointed at Danny. “You! You seem to work here. Make some calls and have the Mondo WS-TY4 installed! That’s the same as was used in the Tokyo Olympics. Lightning fast! Just like my boys!”

“Sorry, but I’m just a sports medicine intern,” Danny replied. “I don’t know how...”

“Well figure it out! ASAP! I can’t have Andy and Driz injure their gold medal feet running on this old garbage!”

“Yes, Coach. I apologize. I’ll try.”

“I thought you said you were a sports medicine intern. Can’t you see Andy and Driz just finished a 200? Get their hydration to them immediately!”

Danny nodded, looked about, and spotted a solar powered LionCooler set at precisely 37.5° Fahrenheit. He retrieved two bottles and began to take them across the field to the waiting pair.

“Run,” hollered Coach Tremaine at Danny! “Can’t you see they are losing electrolytes?”

“Sorry!” Danny called over his shoulder as he sprinted across the field.

Andy and Driz yanked the drinks from Danny’s hands the second he arrived. “Don’t be late again,” snarled Andy.

“Have them waiting the moment we finish each 200,” growled Driz.

And with that, they dropped their bottles, toed the line, and raced off on another 200.

Danny hurriedly gathered up the bottles and darted back across the field to meet them when they finished. The two drank, dropped, and ran once more. Back and forth across the field Danny hustled until their practice was completed, not even having a moments rest to help the remainder of the team. Exhausted, he started toward the gate.

"Where do you think you're going?" shouted Coach Tremaine.

"I thought I'd eat and then do my run," Danny replied.

"You? Run?" mocked Andy.

"In those old shoes?" guffawed Driz.

Coach Tremaine shook his head and laughed. "I don't know how things operated around here before. But we have the Olympic Trials Qualifying Meet coming up soon and I need this facility operating at the highest levels. After every practice I need the track swept, the grass trimmed, the gels restocked, and the hydration prepared for tomorrow's workout. Plus, the weights, bands, stretching bars, and medicine balls need to be cleaned, stowed, and locked away."

"But sometimes Coach Bob let me use the track and the equipment after practice," Danny protested.

"Coach Bob isn't here. I am!" Coach Tremaine barked. "I can't have you scuffing up the new elite running surface with those hard rubber soled shoes!"

“The 1980s called,” Andy sneered.

“They want their sneakers back,” Driz finished.

The three of them laughed and walked away.

And so it was for Danny, day after interminable day. Racing about the field meeting Andy’s and Driz’s every need. Cleaning up after them. Then preparing the facilities for the next morning where it all started over again. He left late every night tired, sore, and unappreciated.

But even though he was no longer allowed to run on the new Mondo WS-TY4 surface, he still found time to practice. The gate to the abandoned junior high school track across town was always open. And even though it was dark, he still ran all the drills Coach Bob had taught him. When he opened up his stride and really pushed the pace for a full mile, he saw in the shadows alongside him deer helping to keep him on pace. In those moments he felt free as the wind streamed across his face. In the pounding of his heart during strength training and drills, he heard the thumping of rabbits' feet from the overgrown infield, helping him sustain his rhythm even as he pushed on to failure. When he flew around the track faster and faster, the birds cheered him on. In those times he knew dreams really were possible if he kept believing, just like Coach Bob always said. His chance would come. He knew it.

Soon it was time for the Olympic Trials Qualifying Meet. Coach Tremaine called all the Emerald Track Club athletes to gather around. "As you know," he began, "tomorrow morning is the Olympic trials qualifying meet. If you podium, you'll advance to the Olympic trials themselves. Win there and you'll be representing our great country at the Olympic games!"

All the runners nodded and clapped. They'd all worked hard for this opportunity, even though Coach Tremaine always seemed to ignore them during practices.

"Of course, we also know," he continued, "that my two stars, Andy and Driz, are going to win everything so it will be a waste of your time to even try! But the rules are the rules, and the rules say I've got to let you all at least take a shot, as hopeless and pathetic as that will be." He glared at the group as they looked dejectedly at the ground and shuffled their feet. "That's what I thought," Coach Tremaine sneered. "Not a one of you with the heart to challenge my boys. If one of you still wants to make a fool of yourself at the meet tomorrow, though, it all starts right here, right now. Toe the line with Andy and Driz, keep up with them for a mile, and maybe I'll let you humiliate yourself in the morning."

Andy and Driz took their positions at the starting line, waiting. "You're all a bunch of losers!" they cackled.

The rest of the team turned away, picked up their gear, and left.

All of them except Danny.

He slipped an Emerald Track Club singlet on over his old threadbare tech shirt and joined the other two.

Andy's mouth gaped, "Coach," he whined, pointing at Danny.

"Not running with him!" Driz agreed, an equally disgusted look on his face.

They looked him up and down in disbelief.

"But your old shorts are disgusting! They hang down almost to your knees!" Andy mocked.

"And under that singlet your shirt is stretched and stained!" complained Driz.

"And what's that all over your horrible shoes?" they taunted in unison. "Are those cinders? Have you been running on some old cinder track and now expect to keep up with us?"

Danny looked at his feet. It was true. He hadn't had a moment to clean the dust and cinders from his feet after his nighttime runs at the old school. He felt his cheeks begin to flush with embarrassment.

"Hey, Cinder Fella," they maligned. "Nobody wants to see you compete!"

Danny ignored them and looked at Coach Tremaine, "You said anybody on the team could run. I'm on the team. My chance has come. I believe. I'd like to try."

Coach Tremaine shook his head. "I did say anybody could try, yes, I did. Anybody on the team."

"You can't be serious!" Andy gasped.

"No way!" Driz agreed.

Coach Tremaine held up his hand to silence the two. Shadows fell across his already darkened eyes as storm clouds began to roll over the horizon. The corners of his lips stretched into an evil smirk. "But, Cinder Fella, you're no longer on this team.

This isn't some fairytale of dreams. You're fired as sports medicine intern!" Lightening flashed and thunder echoed against the nearby hillsides, accentuating his words.

Danny stumbled backward. "But, but..."

"Boys," Coach Tremaine shouted over the growing tumult, "do we ever allow nonmembers to wear a prestigious Emerald Track Club singlet?"

"They are for elites," Andy sneered. "And you, Cinder Fella ... you ..."

"... you're not elite," Driz finished.

And with that, they ripped the singlet off him and threw it to the ground.

Danny, stunned, turned and sprinted away into the thickening gloom. He ran blindly clear across town until finally he found himself back on the cinder track gazing into the darkness.

"I don't understand," he said to the shadowy shapes of his animal friends who were waiting for him to start his practicing. "I kept up my training, here with all of you. I fought through the difficult times when Coach Tremaine treated me so badly, and I never gave up hope. So why did my chance get stolen from me?"

His friends seemed to sense the distress in his voice. They inched closer, eyes wide and caring.

"I'm never going to have this opportunity again. The Olympic Trials Qualifying Meet is once in a lifetime." Danny covered his face with his hands.

As the storm blew past, and the night drifted slowly by, the deer massaged against his legs, the bunnies nuzzled his plantar fascia, and the birds sang Eminem's Lose Yourself.

"Duuuude," came an unfamiliar voice as the dawn began to glow on the horizon.

Danny looked up, startled.

"Duuude, are those little guys like your spirit animals?" the voice came again.

"What?"

"That is totally righteous. Mine is the banana slug. That's right, the ariolimax costaricensis. Oozing along through the world. Completely Zen. But I just have the one. How sweet that you have three."

"Wait. What are you talking about? These aren't spirit animals. They're," he paused for a moment considering. "I guess they're my friends. My three only friends."

"Awesome! My name's Bodhi. Might be a day to bump that number up one. We shall see!"

Danny stood, confused. "I'm, uh, I'm Danny."

"I so utterly knew that! You are fortunate indeed, slender man! But I'm compelled to inquire, with friends times three, why are you so down in the mouth?"

"Down in the what?"

"You know, glum, dispirited, melancholy ... what is raining bleakness on your otherwise rainbow parade?"

"Oh that," Danny whispered. "I wanted to run in the Olympic Trials Qualifying Meet, but Coach Tremaine won't let me."

"Won't let you? Dude, who made him your personal villain? He probably doesn't even have a spirit animal!"

"But he runs the team and ..."

"So, find another team! One that's more chill."

"But the race is in a few hours. I can't ..."

Bodhi unzipped his tattered backpack. From inside a light sparkled.

Danny pointed, "Did you leave your flashlight on in there?"

"Oh, that? Just my mojo." Bodhi winked and reached his hand inside, pulling out a piece of glistening white paper. "Dude, you could join Team Bodhi. I have an entry to the Olympic Trials Qualifying Meet right here!" He shook the page causing glitter to sprinkle to the grass.

Danny's jaw dropped, "That's not possible ... is it?"

"Totally! Dreams grow when you hold onto hope. So, what say you?"

Danny took the entry form and studied it. "This is real! I'm in!"

"Sweet!" Bodhi reached back into the shimmering confines of his pack. "And Team Bodhi members get to wear some thoroughly bodacious threads." He pulled out a brand-new singlet and shorts along with a pair of custom made, specially designed racing flats. All in Danny's perfect size.

Danny tried them on, marveling at the perfect fit. "I feel so fast in these, even just standing here! Are they magic?"

“Nah. But you are magic, running man! And to place a gnarly cherry on top,” Bodhi smiled, “your wave rider hat and shades. With these on you’ll be incognito!”

“I can’t thank you enough. You are amazing.”

“Just sharing the love. It’s totally what I do.”

Danny checked his watch. “It’s almost time for the opening ceremonies. You’re going to be my coach, right? Let’s go!”

“No can do, my skinny friend. I regretfully must decline. My journey is in a different direction. But you won’t have to compete alone!” Once again, he reached into his dusty backpack, this time retrieving three matching Team Bodhi windbreakers. “You shall be accompanied by a coach, assistant, and a trainer!”

Danny looked around, confused since they were alone. “Be serious. Who?”

“You’ve got some serious imagination deficit issues. It’s as simple as bibbity,” Bodhi tossed the first jacket at one of the deer, “bobbity,” he tossed the second at a bunny, “boo!” The third jacket landed on top of a surprised little bird.

In an explosion of glitter and rainbows the three animal companions morphed into the quintessential coaching staff, each wearing full track uniforms and the Team Bodhi windbreakers.

Bodhi clapped extra sparkle dust from his hands and picked up his backpack. “Sweet! My work here is complete! I might have helped you look the part, but once you’re in the race, it’s all up to you! And remember, magic like this is very temporary. Once the race is over, dude, this is finito! Only your hard work will last.”

Danny stood in disbelief, nodding at every word Bodhi was saying.

“Now party on and rip up that course!” And with that, Bodhi strolled away into the underbrush.

Danny waved, smiling. Then he paused and looked to his coaching staff. "Wait," he swiveled his head. "Wait! How am I supposed to get there? Isn't there supposed to be a shuttle or something? Maybe a carriage?"

The coaching team shrugged.

"Could've been," Bodhi called over his shoulder. "Next time bring a pumpkin! For today, might I suggest you just run?"

The assistant tightened the laces of Danny's shoes. The trainer gave him a Vanilla Bean GU. The Coach checked the time, blew his whistle, and pointed toward the gate.

Danny started toward the Olympic Trials Qualifying Meet across town, speeding up with each step. When he arrived, he could scarcely believe his eyes. The track was filled with sprinters, hurdlers, and distance runners. Olympic, university, and club banners made the infield look like a colorful county fair. And in the midst of it all, dressed in red, white, and blue blazers, strode the entire coaching staff of the national Olympic track team, led by the world-renowned Coach Stanley.

As Danny checked in at the gate, he watched Coach Stanley from afar milling among the athletes. The coach shook hands and greeted each person respectfully, but he didn't seem to be very happy. It was as if he was hoping for something, or someone, more.

"But what more could he want?" Danny thought. "You could not ask for better athletes than these!"

At that moment, one of the national staff members pointed in Danny's direction. Soon, all heads turned, and a murmur spread throughout the crowds. "Who is that?" some asked. "I don't recognize him from any other races," others said. "He has a full coaching staff; he must be someone important!" still others surmised.

It took several moments for Danny to realize they were all talking about HIM! At first, he wanted to run back out the gate and get away from their gawking stares. But his coach, assistant, and trainer prodded him forward instead. With no other choice, he held his head high and acted as if he belonged.

Danny went through his warmup routine off to the side, away from the other milers. He didn't want to bump into Andy or Driz for fear of being recognized. He scanned the crowd constantly, just to be safe. It was then he noticed from across the sea of faces that Coach Stanley was watching him! And not just watching, but making his way through the infield toward him!

Danny felt frantic, "What do I do? He probably knows I don't belong here! I probably stand out! If he throws me out, then I'll never fulfill my dream of competing in the Olympics!" His crew shrugged and looked about uncertain.

Fortunately, before he could be discovered and removed from the track, the loudspeakers announced the start of the mile race. Danny yanked off his sweats and hustled to the starting line, safe from Coach Stanley but face to face with Andy, Driz, and Coach Tremaine!

"You're my stars," Coach Tremaine said to Andy and Driz. "None of these other losers can come close to you!"

Andy and Driz pushed their way through the other milers and took lanes 1 and 2. “Make way for the medalists, you bunch of losers,” Andy barked.

“You don’t even belong on the same track as us!” Driz goaded.

Danny kept his head down and stayed near the back of the pack, not wanting to be seen, forgetting that in his new running kit he was unrecognizable.

Coach Stanley hurried toward the line just as the runners were called to their marks. "Wait!" he shouted, pointing at Danny. "Who are you?" But he was too late. The starter's pistol fired.

Andy and Driz immediately broke out in front of the field, stretching to an early lead. Danny, in the meantime, was boxed against the rail in the rear. He wasn't sure what to do. Despite all his training, he'd never been in a real race. As the first of the four laps rushed to a close, he was well behind the leaders.

Danny saw movement along the infield grass beside him. It was his animal friends, now his coaching team, bounding, hopping, and running awkwardly on their new human legs, bleating, whistling, and chirping encouragement. As he rounded turn one for the second time, he juked into lane 3 where he found some clear running space and began to move up beside the pack! And as half the race was finished, he was in front of almost everybody. Only Andy and Driz remained but they were so far ahead, things seemed hopeless.

In that instant, when things seemed impossible, Danny remembered the words of Coach Bob, "You keep up your training, fight through the hardships, and never give up hope. Sometimes dreams do come true!" He redoubled his efforts, dug deep, and began cutting into the gap between him and his two haughty competitors.

With everyone at the meet cheering encouragement, by the end of the third lap, he'd caught them!

"Who ... are ... you?" Andy gasped as Danny pulled alongside. "I ... know ... all ... the ... elites!"

"Impossible ... you ... caught ... us!" Driz gurbled.

"Everything's possible," Danny replied, "with hard work and hope." And with that, he sprinted past!

Andy and Driz tried to speed up, opening their strides and increasing their turnover. But this only caused them to get out of rhythm. Their feet tangled and they fell into a heap on the track, quickly passed by the rest of the competitors.

Danny continued to stretch his lead. He powered through the final turn and down the homestretch, easily winning the race in an impressive 3:47. The crowd roared their approval and Danny became lost in the moment...

... until a firm hand grasped his shoulder. It was Coach Stanley in his official national Olympic team colors. "You!" He said firmly. "Who are you? I know all the contenders and you weren't on my list!"

Danny flinched. "I, uh... I..." he backed away, not wanting to get into trouble.

"Wait," said Coach Stanley. "How did you run that fast?"

Flanked by his coaching staff, Danny escaped into the crowd.

"Don't go!" Coach Stanley called. "You're amazing!"

Coach Tremaine, with Andy and Driz in tow, stepped in front of Coach Stanley. "Don't worry about him," he said. "You saw how well my boys were running before that horrible person tripped them! They deserve a chance on the Olympic team!"

But all Coach Stanley could see was Danny, disappearing through the throng.

Danny, having reached the far side of the field, leaned against a fence. "We did it, guys!" he said to his coaching team. "We won the race!"

They smiled and nodded. His deer coach began massaging against his legs, his bunny assistant nuzzled his plantar fascia, and his trainer began to whistle Eminem's Lose Yourself.

"I, uh, I can't say I've ever seen that post-race cool down routine before," Coach Stanley said, stepping up from the side. "But I don't think it violates any international restrictions. Son, you're a hard one to catch up with! Both on the track and after!"

Danny quickly pushed his animal coaches away. "I, uh... I mean, umm, they..."

"It doesn't matter. You are the most amazing prospect I've seen in a long time! You beat a solid group of athletes today. From what I saw today, I think we can slot you into the 1,500- and 5,000-meter events, if you're interested!" Coach Stanley smiled. "Oh, and your incredible coaching team is welcome to come along as well. I'm quite sure none of my staff is willing to do that plantar nuzzling thing..."

Danny gaped at his friends. "Can you believe it? Dreams do come ..." But before he could finish his sentence, he noticed a feather begin to sprout from his trainer's arm. And the hair on his assistant coach's head began to turn bunny soft. His coach's nose started to turn round and black. Danny began to stammer.

"What is it, son? Are you ok?"

"I, uh... I mean, we, umm... have to go. We have to go!" Danny shoved his team away and began to run down the track toward the gate.

"But we just met!" called the coach. "Why leave now?"

"I must go!" shouted Danny. He ran to the gate.

"At least tell me your name! How can I reach you?"

Danny saw his friends' hands and feet begin to return of paws and hooves. He quickly turned into the bushes.

"Please, stop for a moment!"

"Oh no!" Danny gasped as one racing flat fell off his foot and tumbled back down to the track. But he kept running, his clothes returning to tatters, his hat and shades dissolving into nothing.

"Wait!" called Coach Stanley. He picked up the errant racing flat and rushed to the bushes. He looked around but could not see Danny anywhere. "This is all I have left from him," he said, looking down at the racing flat. He saw that it was made in a special way, custom fit to Danny alone. "Somewhere there is the other racing flat like this one," he said. "And when I find it, I will find him, too. Then I will ask him to be on my Olympic team!"

From track to track, from gym to gym, went Coach Stanley. One middle distance runner after another tried to fit his foot inside the custom flat. But none could fit! And so, the Coach moved on.

At last, he returned to the Emerald Track Club.

"He's coming!" shouted Andy.

"At the gate!" screamed Driz.

"Quick!" yelled Coach Tremaine. "Get ready! Whoever can wear that racing flat goes to the Olympic Trials! One of you must be the one to fit your foot into it. No matter what!"

"Welcome back, Coach Stanley." he said. "I have two runners for you to see."

"Wait," replied Coach Stanley. "Aren't these the two that fell during the race?"

"What?" Coach Tremaine scoffed. "You've seen so many runners these past days, you must be confused!"

"Fine," Coach Stanley relented.

First Andy tried to place his foot in the custom racing flat. He grunted and strained, but it just would not fit. Then Driz stepped up to try his foot inside. But again, it didn't work.

"Are there no other middle-distance runners at this track?" asked Coach Stanley.

"None," replied Coach Tremaine. "But surely you still need someone to fill out your team. Andy and Driz ..."

"Then I must go," said Coach Tremaine.

"Maybe there is one more," said Danny, stepping onto the track from the bushes.

"I thought you said there were no middle-distance runners here," said Coach Stanley.

"Him? He's just a former employee. I fired him for incompetence! He doesn't matter!" hissed Coach Tremaine.

"That's just Cinder Fella!" scoffed Andy.

"He's not elite!" laughed Driz.

But all three had a shadow of doubt creep over their eyes.

"Cinder Fella?" repeated Coach Stanley to Danny. "Come here, son."

Danny stepped up to him. The national Olympic coach got down on one knee and readied the custom racing flat.

But just at that moment, Coach Tremaine lunged for the shoe, grabbed it, and tossed it to Andy and Driz. "Destroy this thing! If you two can't go to the Olympics, nobody else will either!"

Andy and Driz took the custom slipper, sprinted across the field, and threw it into the whirring blades of the giant lawnmower which was being used to groom the turf.

"Stop! Wait!" shouted Coach Stanley. But it was too late. The custom racing flat was gone, as was his chance to ever find the mystery runner who had performed so well. "The shoe, it's gone." He turned to Danny. "I'm sorry you didn't get a chance to try it on."

"It's ok," Danny comforted.

"No, no it's not," Coach Stanley replied.

"It's ok," Danny continued, reaching into his backpack, "because I have the other flat!"

"I knew it!" Coach Stanley cried. "You are the one!"

"What?" squealed Andy.

"Not him!" screamed Driz.

"This cannot be!" yelled Coach Tremaine.

But it was too late. Coach Stanley knew that Cinder Fella was the one. He looked him up and down. He did not see the cinders on his shoes or his threadbare shirt. He only saw an elite athlete. "I have found you!" he said.

"And I have found you," said Danny.

And so, Danny and Coach Stanley left for Colorado to train at altitude for the Olympic Trials. And, to prove fairytales do come true, Danny won the gold in both the 1,500 and 5,000 with Coach Bob, back from Tibet, cheering in the stands. He also got his picture on a Wheaties box and lived happily ever after.

Goodnight Runners' Moon

In the hotel room
There was a charging phone with a playlist of tunes,
And a shirt with a bib near containers of Nuun,
And there were laces with knots
Alongside blister-free socks,
And a baggie of Charmin,
And a finicky Garmin,
And new running shoes,

And an assortment of Gu,
And your fifth bathroom gush,
With an echoing flush,
And a stressed cranky roommate whispering "hush."
Goodnight room.
Goodnight lube.
Goodnight charging phone with a playlist of tunes.
Goodnight safety pins in this thickening gloom.
Goodnight sunglasses.
Goodnight shuttle passes.
Goodnight chance to doze.
Goodnight throwaway clothes.
Goodnight quick dry hat.
Goodnight emergency contacts.
Goodnight shower drip.
Goodnight timing chip.
Goodnight shorts.
Goodnight crush.
Goodnight frazzled nerves.
Goodnight breakfast mush.
And goodnight to the roommate grumbling "hush."
Goodnight sleepless bed.
Goodnight pulling out my own hair.
Goodnight runners everywhere.

Printed in Great Britain
by Amazon